The Night Before Valentine's Day

Grosset & Dunlap

To all my February birthday friends,
whom I love dearly—N.W.

To my sweetheart, Jay,
who gave me an engagement ring
twenty years ago on Valentine's Day—H.P.

Text copyright © 2000 by Natasha Wing. Illustrations copyright © 2000 by Heidi Petach.
All rights reserved. Published by Grosset & Dunlap, a division of Penguin Putnam Books for Young Readers,
New York. GROSSET & DUNLAP is a trademark of Penguin Putnam Inc.
Published simultaneously in Canada. Printed in the U.S.A.

Library of Congress Control Number:00055128

ISBN 0-448-42188-7   E F G H I J

The Night Before Valentine's Day

By Natasha Wing
Illustrated by Heidi Petach

Grosset & Dunlap, Publishers

'Twas the night before Valentine's Day,
and all through the town,
children were busy,
not making a sound.

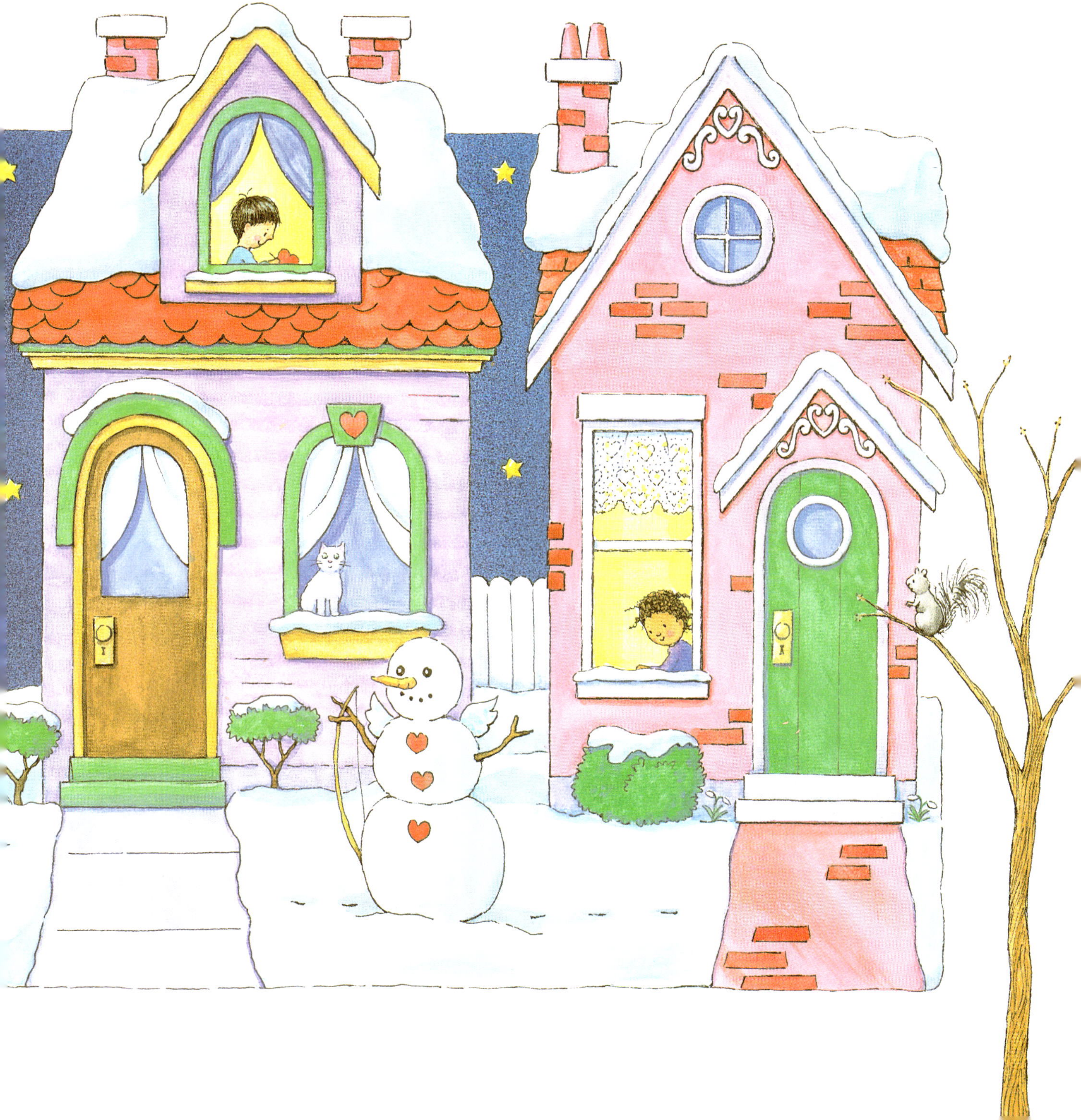

They gathered their scissors,
their glitter and glue,
pink and red paper,
and paintbrushes, too.

They made cards that read,
"Will you be mine?"

and others that said,
"My true valentine."

They trimmed giant hearts
with stickers and lace,

and added an arrow
in just the right place.

Then marking the envelopes
with each friend's name,
they hoped that their friends
were doing the same.

And when they were done,
they slept snug in their beds

while visions of candy hearts
danced in their heads.

The very next morning
it was Valentine's Day!
They grabbed all their cards
and went on their way.

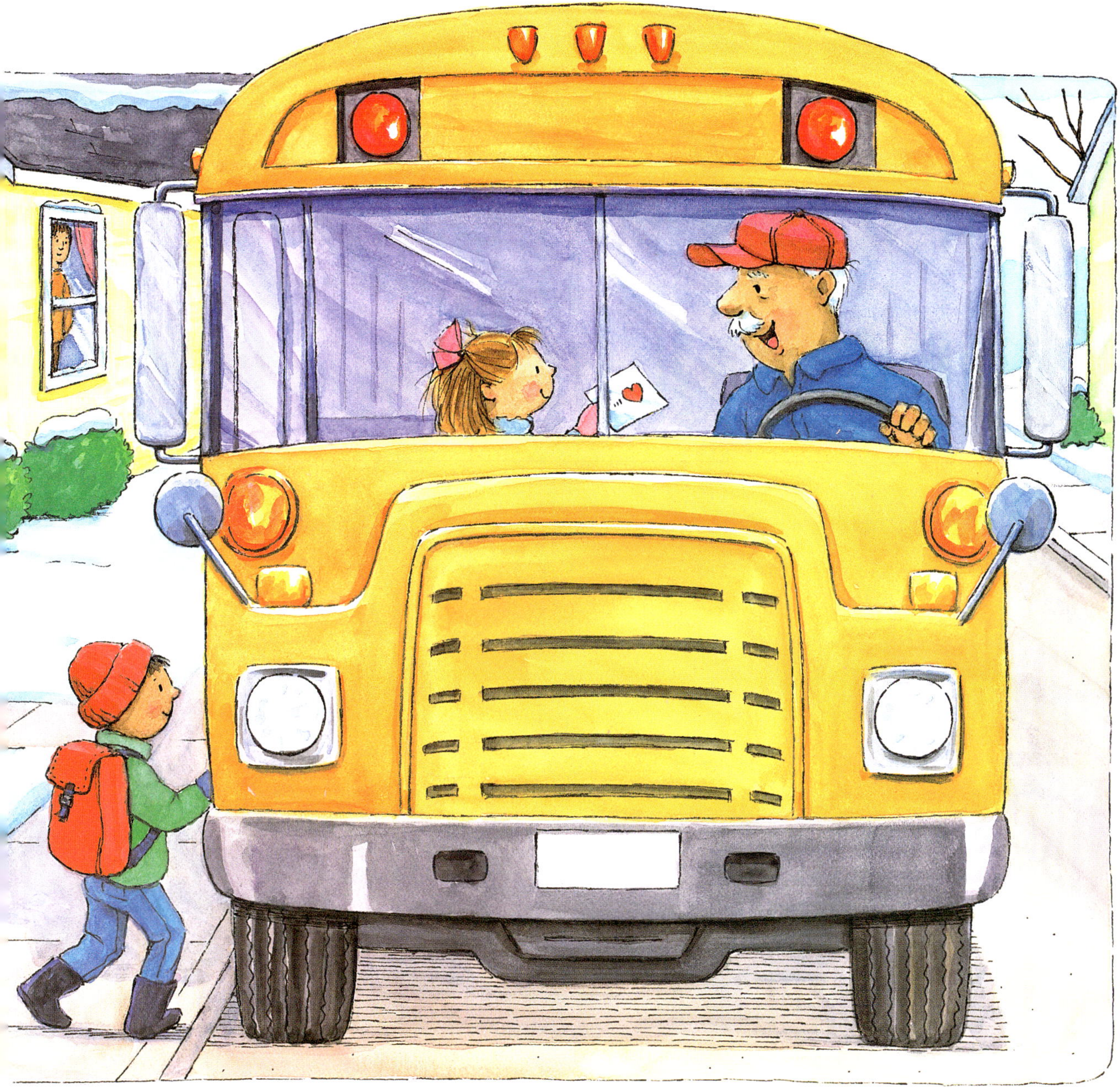

The classroom was decked out
in red, pink, and white,
with balloons and streamers,
so festive and bright.

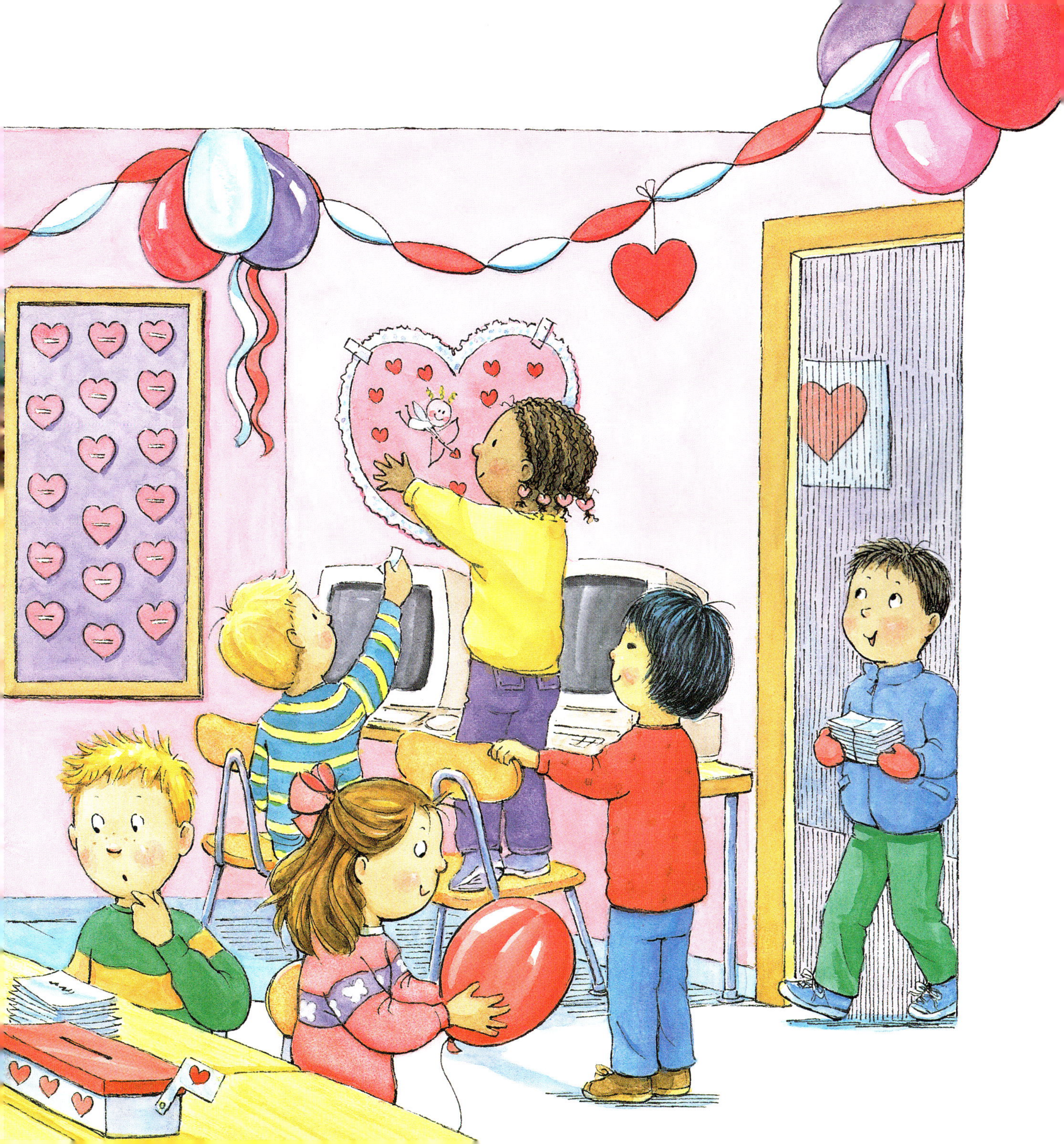

Someone dropped by
with a giant bouquet
addressed to the teacher,
who blushed right away.
The card was signed
"From a secret admirer,"
but everyone knew
it was Mr. O'Meyer!

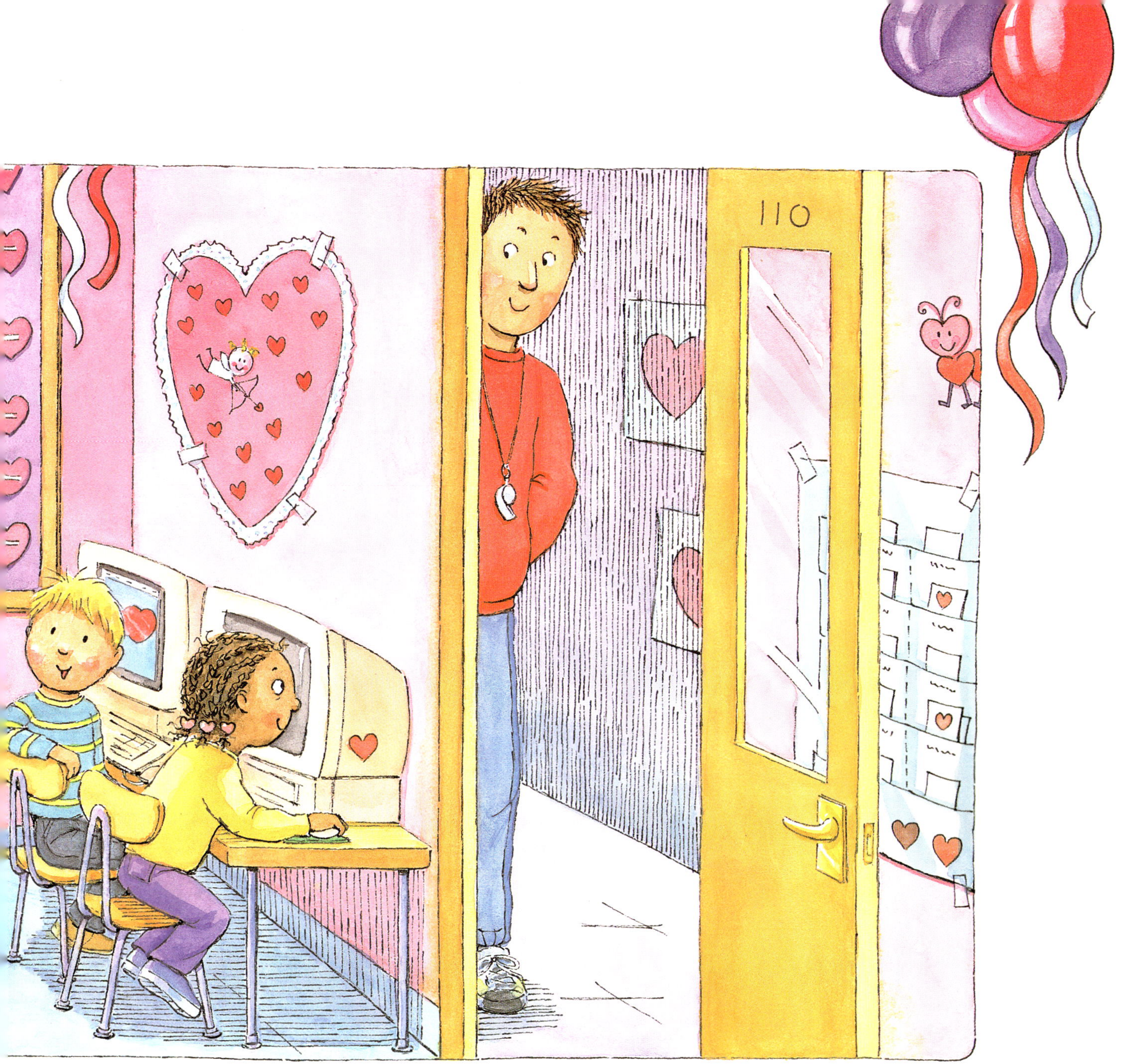
110

They played pin the heart
and won goofy toys,

and girls ran away
from kissy-face boys.

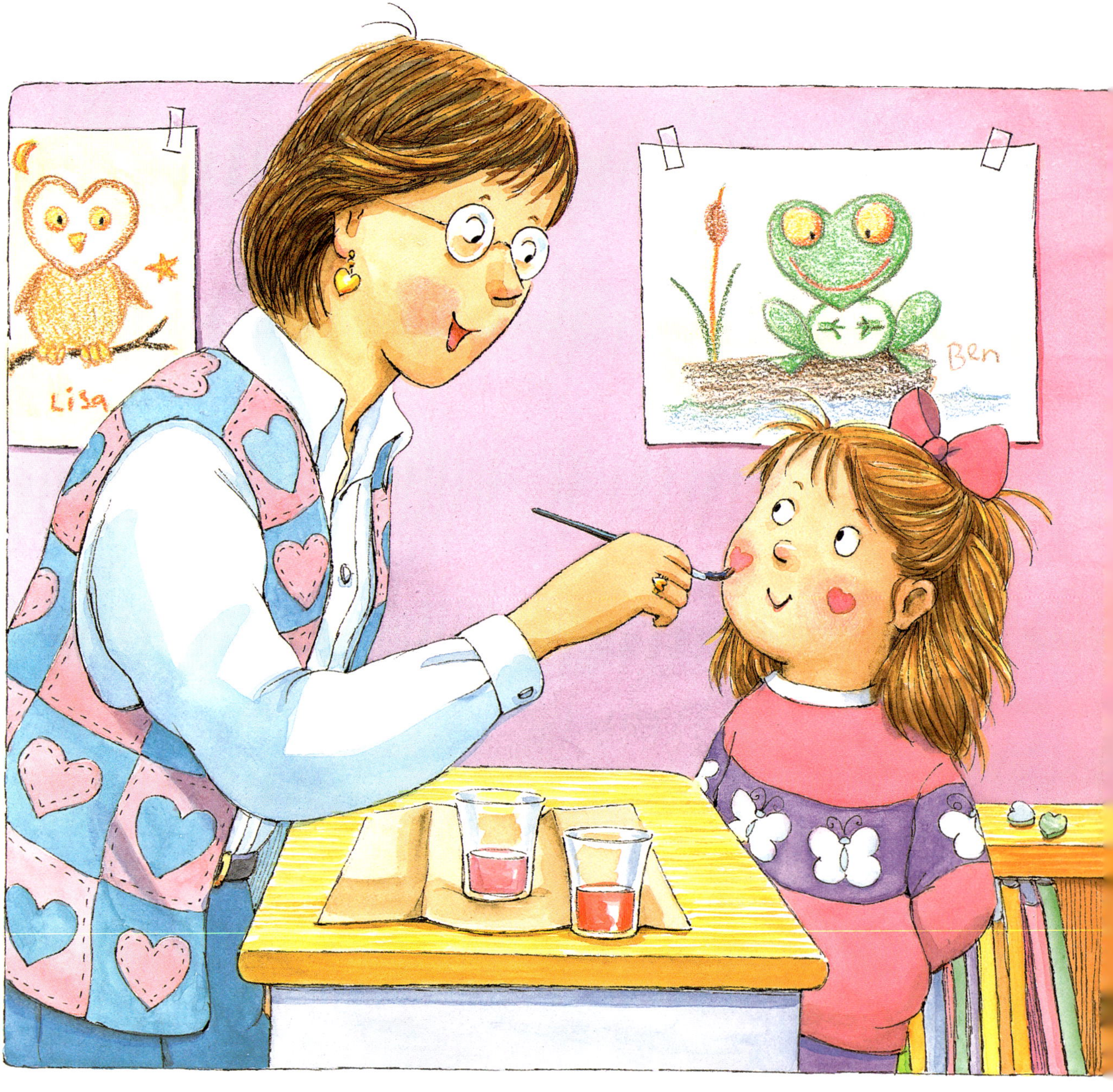
Lisa
Ben

The art teacher came
and painted kids' faces.
She put hearts on cheeks
and sillier places!

At last it was time
to deliver the cards.
Look! One for Lisa,
Jim, and Bernard.

They opened them up,
read them and smiled,
and laughed at the cards
that were totally wild.

Then they ate goodies,
sweet cherries, and grapes,

and drank punch with ice cubes in little heart shapes.

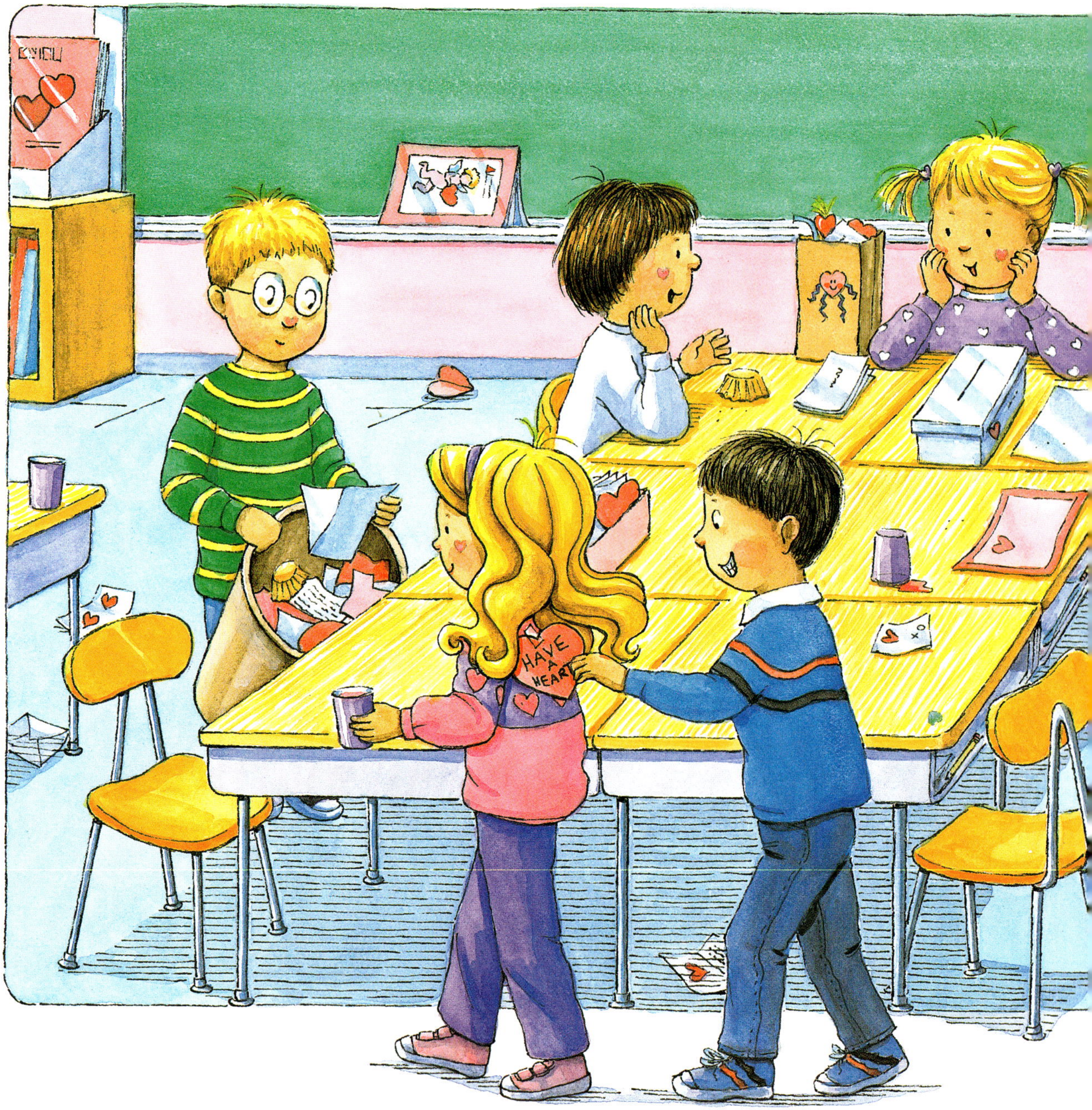
HAVE A HEART

And just when they thought
the party was done,
a knock on the door
came at quarter past one.

When what to their wondering eyes
should appear,
but the principal himself
dressed in full Cupid gear!
His arrows—how golden!
His bow—curved and tight!
The wig that he wore
was a comical sight.

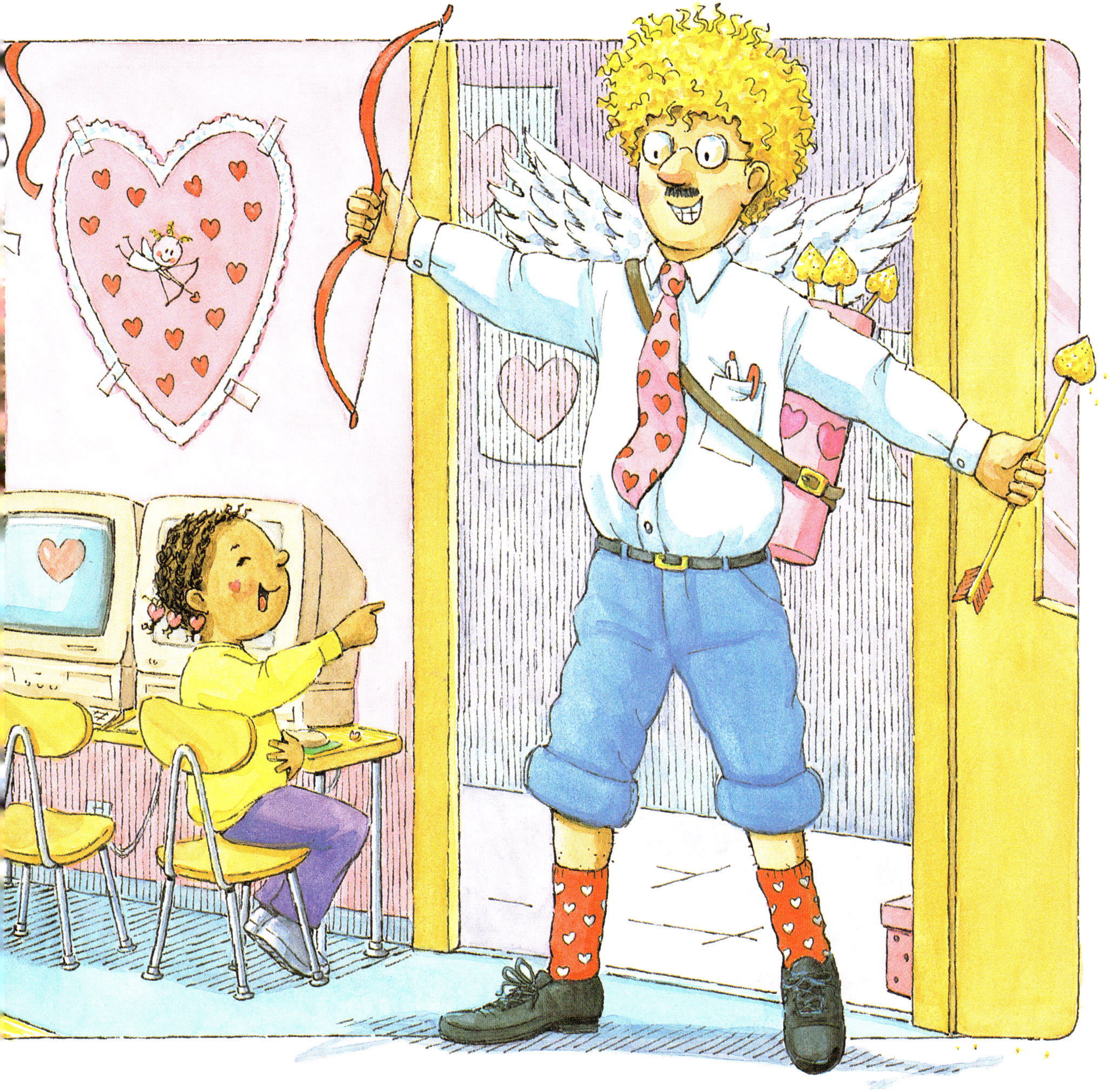

He spoke not a word
and was gone in a minute,
leaving a present behind.
Now what could be in it?

They read Cupid's note
as he leapt down the hall:
"Happy Valentine's Day—
to one and to all!"

Happy Valentine's Day — to one and to all!